THE MAGIC PEACH

First-Start® Legends

THE MAGIC PEACH

A STORY FROM JAPAN

Retold by Janet Palazzo-Craig
Illustrated by Makiko Nagano

Troll

A long time ago, there lived an old man and an old woman. They often wished they had a child to brighten their days.

One day, the old woman was washing clothes in the stream. She heard a noise. *Splish-splash*. To her surprise, a giant peach floated down the stream. She grabbed it. "What a treat this will be!" she said.

That night, the old couple got ready to eat the giant peach. Suddenly, the peach wiggled, jiggled, and split open. Out popped a baby boy!

The old couple's wish for a child had been granted. They called the baby Peach Boy.

Peach Boy was the hungriest baby!
The old couple fed him well. He grew big
and strong. He liked to help his parents
with their work. The old man and the old
woman were happy with their fine son.

11

At that time, some terrible ogres were frightening the villagers and stealing their things. The brave Peach Boy decided to fight the ogres. Before he went, his mother made his favorite dumplings for him to take along. His father gave him a sword and a banner.

Peach Boy set off. Soon he met a dog.
"Where are you going?" asked the dog.

"To fight the ogres," said the boy.

"Those dumplings smell good," said the dog. "If you give me one, I will go with you."

"Very well," said Peach Boy. The dog and the boy set off.

Soon they met a monkey. "Where are you going?" asked the monkey.

"To fight the ogres," they said.

"If you give me a dumpling, I will come with you," said the monkey.

"Very well," said Peach Boy.

The three set off. Soon they met a pheasant. "Where are you going?" asked the pheasant.

"To fight the ogres," they said.

"If you give me a dumpling, I will come with you," said the pheasant.

"Very well," said Peach Boy.

inally, they reached the sea.
They could see the island where
the ogres lived. They climbed into a
boat and rowed to the island.

When they landed, Peach Boy called, "Open the gate! I have come to fight you."

But the ogres only laughed. They would not open the gate. So Peach Boy and his friends thought of a plan.

The pheasant flew over the wall. He pecked at the ogres. Then the monkey climbed over the wall. He unlocked the gate. In rushed Peach Boy and the dog. They joined the fight.

The monkey scratched the ogres. The dog bit them. Peach Boy swung his sword, fighting fearlessly. The ogres were no match for him. At last, the fight was over.

"We give up," sobbed the ogres. They promised to give back all they had taken from the villagers. "We will never bother them again," the ogres said.

Peach Boy and his friends put all the treasures in a cart. They began the trip home.

When they came to the village, cheering people greeted them. The people's treasures were returned to them.

Peach Boy's parents were happy and proud to see him! Peach Boy, his three friends, and his parents went to their little home. And there they lived happily for the rest of their days.

The Magic Peach is one of Japan's best-loved folktales. Many of the folktales of Japan seek to teach children admirable qualities. Peach Boy has many such qualities—he is strong, kind, and helpful to his parents and others.